Treasure Island

Retold by
Angela Wilkes

Adapted by Sam Taplin

Illustrated by
Peter Dennis

Reading Consultant: Alison Kelly
University of Surrey Roehampton

Contents

Chapter 1 The captain's secret   3

Chapter 2 Pirates in the night   12

Chapter 3 The voyage   19

Chapter 4 Danger on the island   26

Chapter 5 Battle and escape   35

Chapter 6 Lost at sea?   41

Chapter 7 Treasure hunt   50

Chapter 8 Home again   57

Chapter 1

The captain's secret

This is the story of my incredible adventure on Treasure Island. I'm Jim Hawkins and I help my mother run the Admiral Benbow Inn...

Each day was just like the last, until the morning a stranger arrived.

I was sweeping, when an old sea captain strode up the road, singing. He saw me and stopped outside the inn.

"Many people here?" he growled. I shook my head. "Then I'll stay," said the captain.

"Name's Billy Bones," he told me, giving me a silver coin. "Look out for a sailor with one leg," he whispered, "and I'll give you a coin every month."

During the day, Billy Bones strode along the cliffs peering at the sea through his telescope. At night, he told scary stories about pirates. He stayed for months, but he never paid my mother a penny.

And old Captain Scar stood alone on the deck with his jagged cutlass in his hand...

One frosty morning, when Billy Bones was out, a man came to the inn.

"Is there a captain staying here?" he asked. Just then, Bones strode through the door. "Hello Bill," said the man. Bones looked as though he had seen a ghost.

Huh?

"Black Dog!" gasped Bones.

"Yes," sneered the man, "and I've come for what's hidden in that sea chest of yours."

You'll never get your hands on it, you interfering devil!

With a clang of steel, both men drew their swords. Bones struck Black Dog on the shoulder and chased him out of the inn.

Bones was so shocked that he grew sick and had to stay in bed.

"You've got to help me Jim," he begged. "Black Dog sailed with a pirate named Captain Flint. Now his whole crew will be after me."

Only a few days later, I heard an odd noise outside. Tap... tap... tap... A blind man was trudging along, tapping the road with his stick.

"Where am I?" he asked.

"The Admiral Benbow Inn," I replied.

The man grabbed my arm with an icy hand. "Take me to Billy Bones," he hissed.

When Bones saw the blind man, he was horrified. The man gave Bones a note and hurried away.

With trembling fingers, Bones read the message. "The pirates!" he gasped. "They're coming tonight!" With a cry of pain, he fell to the floor. To my horror, he was dead.

Chapter 2

Pirates in the night

I didn't like the sound of those
pirates at all. But Mother was
determined to see what Bones
had hidden in his chest. So, that
night, I locked all the doors and
windows of the inn and we went
to the captain's room.

His chest was full of old clothes and weapons, but at the very bottom we found papers and a bag of gold.

Excitedly, we began to count the money. Just then, someone rattled the door of the inn. Then I heard a faint tapping. Tap... tap... tap...

We grabbed the money and papers and ran out into the night.

I'd only just pulled my mother into a hiding place when a gang of men rushed to the inn and smashed down the door. They stormed through our home, shouting, "Bones is dead! Find the papers!"

Suddenly the blind man threw open a window.

"The papers have gone!" he shrieked. "Find the boy!"

But as the pirates came closer to our hiding place, a group of soldiers galloped over the hill.

The pirates fled.

"We heard you were in danger," the captain of the soldiers said to me. "Sorry we took so long."

"The pirates wanted these papers," I explained. "I think we should take them to the Hall and show Squire Trelawny."

Squire Trelawny was having dinner with his friend Dr. Livesey. They were amazed by my story.

When Dr. Livesey opened the packet of papers, he found a map.
"No wonder Flint's pirates

wanted this," he said. "It shows where his treasure is buried!"

Squire Trelawny was thrilled. "Here's my plan," he said. "We shall sail to that island and find Flint's treasure. And you, Jim, can come with us!"

But don't tell anyone about the treasure.

Chapter 3

The voyage

So, a month later, I hugged my mother goodbye and set off to Bristol docks. The Squire looked very excited. "There's our ship," he said. "She's called the *Hispaniola*."

He asked me to take a message to the ship's cook, Long John Silver. I was horrified to see he had only one leg. Was this the sailor Bones had paid me to watch out for? He seemed friendly enough.

Besides, I had something else to worry about.

Captain Smollett, who was in charge of the *Hispaniola*, was angry. "I thought this voyage was a secret," he snapped, "but it seems the whole crew knows you're after Flint's treasure. I don't trust them."

Those sailors are a shifty-looking bunch, if you ask me.

We were all worried by the

captain's news, but it was too late to find a new crew. The next morning, we set sail.

Pieces of eight! Lovely boy!

During the voyage, I made friends with Long John. I liked the talking parrot who sat on his shoulder.

But one night, I was climbing into a barrel to get an apple...

Almost got it.

...when I overheard Long John whispering to a young sailor. "I was Captain Flint's second-in command," he said. "Join us pirates and get rich."

Sounds good. What's the plan?

I broke out in a sweat. Captain Smollett was right. Some of the men were pirates.

"We'll wait until we have the treasure," continued Long John, "then we'll kill the captain and his friends."

Just then there was a cry of "Land ahoy!" Everyone rushed onto the deck to look at Treasure Island.

I ran to the captain's cabin and told everyone what I'd heard.

"We can't give up now!" said the captain. "We must find out who's on our side and be ready to fight."

Chapter 4

Danger on the island

Next morning, we arrived at the island. The men wanted to lie on the beach. Instead, they had to mend sails and scrub the decks. The sailors started grumbling.

Captain Smollett, scared they'd rebel, gave them the afternoon off.

The sailors eagerly rowed for the shore. I was desperate to go too, so I slipped into one of the boats.

When we reached the beach, I jumped out and ran off into the trees.

I can't wait to explore!

I was exploring the island when I heard Long John Silver talking to one of the sailors.

The sailor turned and ran. With a growl, Long John hurled his walking stick, knocking the man down and killing him.

I ran away into the forest, stumbling and gasping.

He killed him!

But then I saw a shadowy figure dodge behind a tree.
As I drew closer, a wild man sprang out!

Don't hurt me! I'm only poor Ben Gunn.

"My pirate friends left me here to die," said Ben. "Please help me escape from the island. I'll make you rich if you do."

Just at that moment, the distant boom of a cannon shook the air.

Meanwhile, as I found out later, Dr. Livesey was searching for me with one of the sailors. They came across a fort made of logs on a hill.

Suddenly, they heard a piercing

scream from the ship. "The pirates are attacking," said the doctor. "Quick! We'll get the others and hide here."

The pair rushed back to the ship, helped the captain load a boat with guns and rowed desperately for the shore. Some pirates fired at them with the ship's cannon, but they reached the land safely.

So, as I ran across the island, I saw the captain's flag fluttering over the log fort. I scrambled over the fence and dashed inside.

"I've just seen Long John Silver kill a sailor!" I cried, panting. "And when I ran away, I met a man called Ben Gunn in the woods!"

"Silver killed a sailor?" said the Squire, looking worried.

"We don't have many guns," added Dr. Livesey, "and the pirates are fierce fighters."

We stayed up all night, trying to decide what to do. But, as the sun came up, we still didn't have a plan.

Chapter 5

Battle and escape

At dawn, Long John Silver came hobbling up the hill. "Give us the treasure map," he said, "and we won't harm you."

"We don't bargain with pirates," said the captain.

"Then you're all dead men," sneered Long John and walked off.

35

The captain looked at us.

"Get ready to fight, my lads," he said. Time seemed to stop. It became very hot and quiet.

Suddenly, shots rang out and pirates swarmed over the fence. The captain's men opened fire and a savage battle began.

Finally, the fighting was over and the last few pirates ran off, defeated. Dr. Livesey took the treasure map and disappeared into the woods.

I guessed he had gone to find Ben Gunn and I wanted to help. Taking two pistols, I crept away to join him.

But, as I walked along the beach, I found a boat Ben Gunn had made. It gave me a wonderful idea. I would cut the *Hispaniola* loose from its rope. With luck, the few pirates left on board would be taken by surprise and the ship would run aground!

I'll give those pirates something to think about.

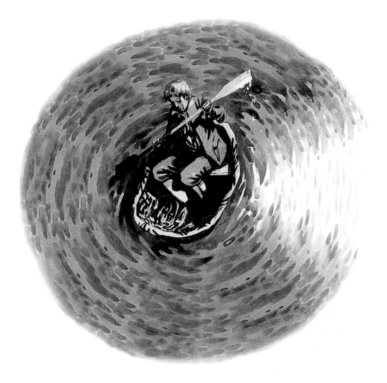

It was easy to launch the little
boat into the waves, but it wasn't
so easy to steer it. When I tried to
paddle, the boat just spun in circles.

Luckily, the tide swept me over
to the ship. Catching hold of the
anchor rope, I sliced through it.

I could hear people shouting inside, so I quietly crawled up to a window. Two pirates were locked in a vicious fight.

The ship moved suddenly, startling the pirates. I dived back into my boat and crouched at the bottom. I hid, with my eyes shut, as the waves carried me out to sea.

Chapter 6

Lost at sea?

Hours later, I woke with my head spinning. It was already daytime and I was bobbing on the sea not far from the island. But, when I tried to paddle ashore, the boat was caught by a huge wave and plunged underwater for a second.

41

I was terrified. I realized I had no control over the boat and feared I'd be lost at sea forever. Then, to my great relief, I saw the *Hispaniola* drifting my way. There was only one thing to do. I would have to get on board and try to take charge.

All of a sudden, the ship reared up on the sea and towered over me. I sprang up and managed to catch hold of it, just as it smashed the little boat to tiny pieces.

Holding on with all my strength, I clambered along a mast as the ship rocked and plunged.

Gently, I swung myself down onto the deck. The whole place seemed strangely quiet.

In a corner, two pirates were lying in a pool of blood. One was dead, but the other groaned and looked up. It was Israel Hands, one of Long John Silver's friends.

Hands smiled slyly. "I'll help you sail the ship to the island if you like," he offered.

But as we approached a bay, I heard a noise behind me. I whirled around. Hands was clutching a dagger, ready to strike.

What are you doing?

Getting the ship back!

He lunged at me, but I skipped to one side. Then I tried to fire one of the pistols... There was only a dull click.

In desperation, I scrambled up the mast ropes, climbing higher and higher.

You can't escape that easily, lad!

At one point I glanced down. Hands was climbing after me! I paused to reload my pistols.

Suddenly, Hands hurled his

dagger, striking me on the shoulder. I have never felt such pain, before or since.

As I shouted out, both pistols went off. Hands screamed and dropped into the sea.

With a thumping heart and
throbbing shoulder, I climbed down
and swam ashore. I'd escaped. And
now the *Hispaniola* was ready for
the captain. Eagerly, I set off
across the island to find my friends.

When I finally
reached the log
fort, it was dark.
I crept inside,
stumbling in
the gloom.

Suddenly, a weird voice shrieked,
"Pieces of eight!" It was the parrot.
I tried to run, but someone
grabbed me and held up a light.

Chapter 7

Treasure hunt

To my dismay, I was surrounded by pirates!

"Your friends have gone," Long John said. "There's only us now." Another pirate snarled and lunged at me with a knife. "Hey!" growled Long John, "I'm in charge here."

The pirates glared at him. "We want a new leader," one of them said. Long John took something out of his pocket and held it up.

Everyone gasped: Flint's treasure map! I was puzzled, but Long John wouldn't tell me how it came into his hands.

Next morning, to my surprise, Dr. Livesey arrived. He'd agreed to look after the wounded pirates.

Long John was determined to keep me a prisoner, but he let me talk to the doctor for a while.

"I thought you'd gone," I said, telling Dr. Livesey about my adventure on the *Hispaniola*.

Well done, Jim! Don't worry, we'll rescue you.

Soon after breakfast, the pirates set off to find the treasure. They took me with them.

The map said Flint's chest was buried under a tall tree in the shadow of Spyglass Hill.

How will I ever escape?

As we neared the spot marked "X" on the map, a pirate up ahead began to shout. But he hadn't found treasure... He'd found a skeleton.

In the silence that followed, a spine-chilling voice filled the air. It sang a sailor's song. "The ghost of Captain Flint!" cried the pirates.

"Don't be stupid," said Long John. "It's just someone trying to scare us."

Another pirate spotted a tall tree and everyone charged over to it. But at the bottom of the tree was an empty hole. The treasure had gone.

Long John tapped me on my good shoulder. "There's going to be trouble," he whispered. Was he on our side now?

I clutched my pistols tightly, feeling sweat run down my neck.

The men are going to be furious. Get ready to fight.

Chapter 8

Home again

The pirates stared at Long John menacingly and drew their guns. Just then, shots rang out. Dr. Livesey and Ben Gunn charged out of the bushes with a sailor named Gray. The terrified pirates ran off.

"Quick!" said the doctor. "We must get to the boats before the pirates." We sprinted to the beach, with Long John hobbling behind.

"Don't leave me!" he panted. "The others will kill me."

I'll damage this boat, so the pirates can't follow us.

We clambered aboard a boat and rowed for the *Hispaniola*.

As Gray rowed, Dr. Livesey cleared up a mystery. "I tricked Silver with the treasure map," he told me. "I wanted to distract the pirates. I knew Ben had found Flint's treasure years ago."

Leaving Gray behind to guard the *Hispaniola*, the rest of us headed for Ben's cave and the treasure.

The Squire and Captain Smollett are waiting for us in Ben's cave.

Ben's cave was enormous. The ground was covered in huge heaps of glittering coins, gold bars and jewels that gleamed in the firelight.

The Squire and Captain Smollett were thrilled to see me. That night, we had a grand feast to celebrate finding Flint's treasure.

Next morning, we loaded up the ship with the treasure and sailed away. We took Long John along, but during the voyage, Ben Gunn helped him escape with some gold.

"I thought we'd be better off without him," Ben said.

When we landed at Bristol docks, I hugged everyone goodbye and took my share of the gold. I never saw Long John Silver again.

I never did go back to Treasure Island, but sometimes, in my dreams, I hear the waves on the sand or Long John's parrot squawking, "Pieces of Eight!"

Try these other books in
Series Two:

The Fairground Ghost: When Jake goes to the fair he wants a really scary ride. But first, he has to teach the fairground ghost a trick or two.

The Incredible Present: Lily gets everything she's ever wished for... but things don't turn out as she expects.

Gulliver's Travels: Gulliver sets sail for adventure and finds a country beyond his wildest dreams...

King Arthur: Arthur is just a boy, until he pulls a sword out of a stone. Suddenly, he is King of England. The trouble is, not everyone wants him on the throne.

Series editor: Lesley Sims

Designed by
Katarina Dragoslavić

First published in 2003 by Usborne Publishing Ltd., Usborne House,
83-85 Saffron Hill, London EC1N 8RT, England. www.usborne.com
Copyright © 2003, 1982, Usborne Publishing Ltd.